Joan Carris

illustrated by Noah Z. Jones

D0168050

CANDLEWICK PRESS

For those who care for and protect the animals in our world
J. C.

For Eli
N. Z. J.

Text copyright © 2009 by Joan Carris
Illustrations copyright © 2009 by Noah Z. Jones

First paperback edition 2011

The Library of Congress has cataloged the hardcover edition as follows:

Carris, Joan Davenport.
Wild Times at the Bed and Biscuit / Joan Carris ; illustrated by Noah Z. Jones. — 1st ed.
p. cm.
Summary: Dr. Adam Bender, the veterinarian at the Bed and Biscuit, accepts four sick animals from the wildlife shelter for treatment and tries to make them feel at home, with the help of the domestic animals already there.
ISBN 978-0-7636-3705-7 (hardcover)
[1. Veterinarians — Fiction. 2. Animals — Fiction. 3. Domestic animals — Fiction.
4. Wildlife rescue — Fiction.] I. Jones, Noah (Noah Z.) ill. II. Title.
PZ7.C2347Wil 2009
[E] — dc22   2008938398

ISBN 978-0-7636-5294-4 (paperback)

11 12 13 14 15 16 BVG 10 9 8 7 6 5 4 3 2

Printed in Berryville, VA, U.S.A.

This book was typeset in Ole Claude.
The illustrations were done in pencil and watercolor.

Candlewick Press
99 Dover Street
Somerville, Massachusetts 02144

visit us at www.candlewick.com

Contents

1
Welcome to the Wild Ones

ERNEST THE MINI-PIG stared at the wild Canada goose in the cage. The goose had a pointed stick going all the way through his neck — in one side and out the other — a few inches below his head. He lay motionless, looking at Ernest with dark, hopeless eyes.

Big geese are fierce, Ernest thought. *They chase folks and flap their wings and fight. Not this one, of course. He's in too much pain.*

"Out of the way, Ernest!" called Grampa Bender. "Put those fox kits over in the corner, Terry, next to the goose. Cover both cages with these towels, please, and maybe they'll feel calmer." Grampa left the office in a hurry.

From her perch on the curtain rod, Gabby the mynah bird said to Ernest, "So where's *my* towel? *I'm* not calm! First a giant goose and now foxes. What's the matter with that man?" She clacked her strong orange beak in disapproval.

Ernest looked up at her. "Remember? The wildlife shelter is having new pens built. This is the day we get all their problems."

"We don't get any nice boarders? We just get the problems?" Gabby flew down onto Grampa's desk and began preening her dark purple and green feathers. Gabby preened whenever she was upset.

Today, everyone at Grampa's place was either upset or anxious. Instead of boarding the usual tame animals like dogs, cats, and birds, the Bed and Biscuit was temporarily going to care for some wild creatures. Because he was a veterinarian, Grampa Bender had volunteered to care for any animals from the wildlife shelter who were sick.

Carefully he backed into the office with a third cage, smaller this time. In it was a furry, smelly, dark brown creature a bit bigger than a rabbit. It had a large head and twitching whiskers. On seeing Ernest, it gave an angry squeal.

"Be nice to our muskrat, Ernest," Grampa said as he set its cage next to the others in the corner. "He's got an infected foot, so he's in a bad mood."

"Old Man Musky is always in a bad mood," said Terry. "But he's been at the shelter since he was born, so we love him anyway. And now — with that bad foot — I'm sure glad he's here, Doc."

Ernest made a few reassuring oinks for the thing called a muskrat. The muskrat squealed twice and turned its back on him.

"I wish *I* had your confidence in me." Grampa smiled at Terry. "I haven't ever treated a muskrat, but he'll be in one of my textbooks. And I can call my old buddies from vet school if I need to."

Grampa Bender took off his gold-rimmed glasses and rubbed his eyes, as he often did when he was thinking hard. "I'll work with the goose first, but I sure don't like the look of those fox kits. How long you reckon they've been orphans?"

Terry shook his head. "We can only guess. Red fox kits are born in the spring, so by this time in the fall these kits should be foraging on their own—a couple of healthy teenagers hunting in open country, know what I mean?"

"Know what I mean?" echoed Gabby.

Terry did a double take. "Whoa, Doc! That bird's amazing!"

"That bird's amazing!" Gabby repeated, sounding exactly like Terry.

Grampa said, "She's a Vietnamese hill mynah. They're the best mimics in the world, far as I know. Be a garbage truck for us, Gabby, please."

Delighted to be asked, Gabby made the sound of a garbage truck digesting its load of trash. After the clanking and crunching noises, she did the *beep-beep* warning as her imaginary truck backed up.

Ernest gave a soft *wrunk* of appreciation for Gabby's talent.

When he quit laughing, Terry said, "Cute little pig, too. You've got a great place here, Doc. You won't be stuck with our animals for long — one or two weeks, tops. The pond will be dredged by then, the new cages finished — we'll be back in business." He and Grampa went outside.

Gabby repeated, "Cute little pig. Cute little pig," and cackled noisily.

Ernest fumed. No male pig wants to be little. He wants to be impressive, forceful, awesome. Not small, and above all, *not cute*.

"Big-mouth bird!" he gibed. She hated her outsize beak as much as he hated being very small. Before she could retort, he said, "I'm going to find Milly and tell her what's going on. And Sir Walter. We can't have him bothering that goose . . . or these fox kits!"

"Wait for me!" Gabby lit on Ernest's head, her regular seat on the pig.

"Mind the claws!" Ernest said, wincing. He wiggled through the pet door and descended the steps with slow care. Like all pigs, Ernest viewed steps with some alarm.

He scanned the low, white building on the left, where cats boarded. Milly often visited there, cheering the boarders with gifts of fresh field mice. Today she lay dozing in the sun next to the outdoor run of a huge Maine coon cat named Trapper.

Gabby eyed Trapper and flapped to the top of a nearby tulip tree.

Milly woke with a wide, pink yawn.

Ernest waited until she opened her eyes. "The wild boarders are here," he said. "One's a Canada goose. Great big goose, with a mean-looking pointy stick going right through his neck! Grampa calls it an arrow. We got two fox kits — runty little things with bad fur. They're scared. And we got a muskrat thing with a wounded foot and a hot temper."

"That's much more trouble than boarding a few nice cats!" Milly replied. She bent her head down to lick the spotless white circle on her chest. All of her fur, which was mostly a dark orange-marmalade color, glistened with health.

"How long will they be here?" she asked. "I have a full-time job now, you know, taking care of Grampa, catching mice, keeping an eye on that hyperactive puppy . . . I could go on for *hours.*"

Milly slept with Grampa and washed his ears daily whether he wanted them washed or not. She also washed Sir Walter, the Scottie puppy, who liked the attention but squirmed a great deal during bath time.

Just then, the puppy exploded from the house, the pet door banging behind him. Racing toward them he barked, "Yarp, yarp! I can play, I can play! Let's chase chickens!"

Grampa called out, "Ernest! Milly! Keep the puppy with you. Stay here in the yard, you hear me? STAY!" He pointed firmly at the large grassy square between the house and the red-brick office building.

"You hear me? STAY!" Gabby echoed from her branch.

Sir Walter jumped up to nibble Ernest's ear with eager puppy teeth.

"Where's your chewy bone?" Ernest leaned his head down toward the puppy so that the

chewing hurt less. He didn't really mind, to be honest. Sir Walter had survived a raging fire and his mother's death. He was healthy now, and happy. Everyone spoiled him, especially Ernest and Grampa.

"Let's play chase," Sir Walter said when he quit chewing on Ernest.

"Pigs don't play chase," Ernest said gravely. "Milly and Gabby will play with you."

"Not this birdy," Gabby warbled.

"I'll play, but no biting, and I mean it," said Milly. Like many cats, she disliked dogs, but Sir Walter had shown himself to be both brave and loving. No one could resist him for long. Also, she was barely more than a kitten herself, and she loved to run.

Sir Walter bounced up and down, ready to race. Milly took off in a red-gold flash, and the puppy tore after her, round and round inside the big square of grass. Ernest flopped down to rest under the branch where Gabby perched and dozed in the warmth of late morning.

Ernest found he could not relax. His mind kept showing him pictures of that pathetic goose. How could he eat with that arrow in his neck? Eating was important to Ernest. He was happiest when he had a full stomach and just plain miserable when he was hungry.

Ernest thought about Old Man Musky with his strong smell, big teeth, and bad temper. And the red foxes. He and Grampa had learned about foxes from a TV program. Humans hunted them for sport and for their beautiful red pelts. Yet foxes were smart. They ran fast, hid well, and were good hunters themselves.

But not ours, Ernest decided. *Our foxes are babies and they're sick.*

And then there was Sir Walter. Since he had begun acting like a normal puppy, Ernest had most often been his companion. Grampa always told him, "Ernest, you're my puppy-sitter."

And so Ernest sat up, a pig on duty. Napping would have to wait. He could see that the days ahead were going to be very tricky.

2
Wild Problems

AFTER LUNCH, Grampa settled Sir Walter in his basket for a nap and headed for the office. Normally the afternoon was for various routine jobs. Grampa might give a rabies shot or dose an ailing cat. He would order hay, straw, and feed for his stock. Sometimes he mowed the grass or paid bills. Whenever possible, he rode his horse, Beauty. Today, of course, was not a normal day.

Today they had a wild goose in real trouble, a pair of sickly fox kits, and a grouchy muskrat with an infected foot. Grampa had taken only a few regular boarders so that he could care for the wild animals.

With Ernest on his heels, Grampa went to his desk in the waiting room. The anxious fox kits had poked their black noses through the wire netting of their cage and were yipping in a pitiful way.

"I know you two are hungry," Dr. Bender told them, "but I can't feed you till I examine you, and right now that goose comes first."

He punched phone buttons fast. "Hello, AnnaLee?" He described the new wild boarders and offered her a job, working afternoons and Saturdays. "You've been great the other times I needed you, but just say no if you're too busy. You've probably got fifteen boyfriends by now."

AnnaLee laughed. "No boyfriends, Doc. Too much homework. But I can help for a while. I need money for Christmas presents."

"Can you come today?"

Across the room, Ernest heard Gabby visiting with the fox kits. He hoped she was making them feel at home. Grampa told the humans who brought their pets, "This is their home away from home."

Even for the dopey chickens, Ernest thought gloomily. He was a naturally kind and thoughtful pig, yet Grampa's chickens tried his patience. If a chicken had a brain, it was the size of a corn kernel . . . maybe smaller.

Now Ernest went over to Gabby and the fox kits, just to check. No one was ever sure what Gabby would say.

"I'm being very friendly, Your Royal Nosiness," she said. "I told them about the Bed and Biscuit, but all they want is food."

"We're starving," said the smaller kit. She and her sister looked fearfully at Ernest and shrank back into one corner of their cage.

"Back off," hissed Gabby. "You scare them because you're so big."

Ahhh. *So big.* Ernest loved hearing those words. Very softly he said, "The man will feed you after he looks you all over. He is an animal doctor. The best in the world."

"The best!" Gabby wagged her bill up and down.

"Humans are bad," said the larger kit. "We can't stay here. Tell the human to open our cage so we can run away."

"He won't know what I'm saying," Ernest said. "Grampa can't talk pig, and believe me, I've tried."

"Very bad at bird speak, too," added Gabby. "Only fair with horse, dog, and cat speak. Knows a little cow and chicken. Of course, he's *much* better than most humans."

"All humans are bad," the larger kit said again. "They hate foxes. They hunt us and kill us."

"Not here!" Ernest squealed.

"Ernest, please!" said Grampa. "I'm on the phone!"

The littler fox kit took one step out of her corner. "What did he say?"

"He wants me to be quiet so he can hear what AnnaLee is saying. Right, Gabby?"

Gabby fluffed her tail feathers and launched into a lecture on telephones. She ended with, "Ernest and Milly do not use the phone. I do their calling for them." Her every feather quivered with pride.

Again, the smaller kit inched forward. "How do you know what he says?"

"Well, we live in the house with him," Ernest replied. "He talks to us because we're his family. . . . And we watch television. I like learning languages, too. Mainly I know what humans say because I have such a dependable brain."

Both fox kits regarded Ernest with awe and respect.

Ernest sat still, basking in their admiration.

Gabby said, "We're building a stage for Ernest so that he can be seen and heard whenever he lectures. It's behind the barn, *right next to the manure pile!*"

Before Ernest could retort, the larger fox kit said, "You cannot be a family. We're a family. We're both foxes. It's just that we lost our mother and father."

"But we *are* a family," Ernest insisted. "Gramma is dead, so Grampa needs us. He got Gabby first, then me three years ago when my mother died. Last year, he found Milly hiding in our barn. Sir Walter the Scottie is new and he's just a baby."

"We're a *blended family,*" Gabby added haughtily. "You can see other blended families on TV all the time."

A low, sad honk came from the surgery.

"Ye gods, my poor goose!" Grampa said good-bye to AnnaLee and went back into his surgery with Ernest right behind him.

The goose's black head drooped. So still was he that his barred feathers — a stunning mix of light and dark brown — seemed to be painted on. He resembled a wild bird carved by an artist — handsome, yet lifeless.

Grampa bent down to look the goose in the eye. "Don't you dare give up, you great big honker. Give us a chance, okay?"

3
AnnaLee

LATER THAT AFTERNOON, Ernest, Milly, and Gabby gathered at the full-length window beside the office door. One of their favorite humans was coming: sixteen-year-old AnnaLee McBroom, who lived on the neighboring farm. Three years ago she had regularly fed Ernest, cuddling him and singing to him.

Now here she was, in a dark green sweat suit and a white headband, jogging up their lane. Her glossy red ponytail swung from side to side.

Gabby sang, "Here comes Santa Claus, here comes Santa Claus, right down Santa Claus—"

"I don't think so," Milly observed. "Looks like AnnaLee to me."

Sir Walter the Scottie bounced in from outdoors beside Grampa. In the doorway Grampa hugged AnnaLee and ushered her into the waiting room. "Here she is, folks. Our troubles are over."

Panting from her run, AnnaLee knelt beside Ernest. "Oh, look at you! You're such a *big pig* now!" She hugged him.

Ernest closed his eyes in pleasure. *What a smart girl.*

AnnaLee petted Milly, stroked Gabby's feathers, told everyone she loved them, then picked up Sir Walter. "Our miracle doggie. Boy, are you cute!"

Sir Walter had been born prematurely in the McBrooms' barn at the time of the fire. Many neighbors, Grampa among them, had come to fight the fire. After it was extinguished, Grampa had found the mother dog under an azalea bush. She was dead, with her nearly-dead pup beside her. Of course, Grampa had brought the puppy home, hoping to save his life.

Now eight weeks old, Sir Walter was easily excited. He wriggled out of AnnaLee's arms, ran around the room once, and wet the floor.

"Be right back," Grampa said, scooping up the puppy and heading outside. "Looks like we need to have another talk about where to do what."

On returning to the office, Grampa said, "Lots to do, AnnaLee. Goose first."

"I've been looking at him ever since you left, Doc. Why isn't he dead? What are we going to *do*?"

"He isn't dead because that arrow didn't hit anything vital. I can't bear to think about the person who shot him and left him to die. So let's just try to be real calm."

Ernest was torn. He wanted to know what was going on in the surgery, and yet here was Sir Walter, sniffing around the foxes' cage.

The puppy poked his nose under the towel on the cage. "I'm Sir Walter. I'm a dog. Who are you?"

"We're red foxes. Leave us alone."

"What's a red fox?" the puppy asked.

Ernest said, "You folks just visit nicely here. I need to be with Grampa. No barking, Sir Walter. They're sick and they're hungry. Okay?"

Both Ernest and Gabby went into the surgery. Gabby settled on one end of the examining table where she had a good view. Ernest made a few calming *wrunk-wrunk* sounds for the benefit of the goose.

Grampa had a towel over the goose's head. Swiftly he wrapped strips of sheeting around the goose, strapping his wings safely against his body.

"This is one big honker," Grampa told AnnaLee.

"One big honker," echoed Gabby.

"Hold on and don't let go," Grampa whispered.

Before the goose could object, Grampa snipped off the entire portion of arrow with the pointed end. "Good, good, keep him steady," he said as he removed the rest of the arrow in one smooth motion.

"Ahnk," went the goose. He moved his head very slightly right, then left. Right again, then left.

Grampa held his breath and took the towel off the goose's head. Now the goose swiveled his neck more fully.

"He's not struggling anymore," AnnaLee said.

Grampa and the wild goose looked at each other for several seconds. "I'm going to flush out that wound," Grampa told the goose, "then give you an antibiotic, and you're going to get well — or my name isn't Dr. Adam Bender!"

As he cared for the goose, Grampa said, "We'll do the goose first every afternoon, AnnaLee, then food for the foxes, milking, and the fox kits again before you go. I can manage the muskrat. He'll sleep after I operate on his foot, and then he'll eat and sleep some more." Grampa grinned. "I'm boarding just one old dog and two cats, so for a while we can pretend we're a wildlife shelter."

"Isn't it about the same?"

"Oh, no! Wild things are *wild by nature.* That's why I hate to see people try to make pets out of them. So we won't even think about taming the fox kits, not that we could. I don't know anything so determinedly wild as a fox."

As he talked, Grampa unwound the cloth strips so that the goose could move about in his cage. He stroked the silky feathers on the goose's back while AnnaLee put food and water in one corner of the cage. The goose angled his black head to look down at the green plastic matting under him.

"Doc, don't you think he's acting kind of . . . well . . . kind of . . ."

"Sluggish," Grampa Bender finished. "Yes, he is, and I don't like it. But it's early days yet." He draped a sheet over much of the cage and set it on a counter in the corner.

"He's magnificent, isn't he? Like a king," AnnaLee said. "Oh, hey! Let's call him Zeus!"

"Zeus the goose? Don't let the goose Zeus loose!" Grampa chuckled at his own joke.

With a tilt of her head, Gabby muttered, "Loose goose Zeus. Foose poose on Zeus."

Birds, Ernest thought.

4
Ernest Becomes a Parent

WITH THE GOOSE TEMPORARILY settled, Grampa asked AnnaLee to bring the fox kits into the surgery.

"Hoo, Doc, they're light as a feather," AnnaLee said as she brought in the cage of tiny foxes. Sir Walter followed, right on her heels.

"No, Laddie," Grampa told the puppy. "We can't watch you and work at the same time." He nudged him away with one gentle, booted foot.

Sir Walter turned to gnaw on the boot.

Grampa pointed to the waiting room. "Ernest, take the puppy out there."

Ernest snouted the puppy away from Grampa, who shut the door to the surgery. Out

in the waiting room, Ernest said, "So, what do you think of the red fox kits?"

"They don't like me," Sir Walter told him.

"How do you know?"

"They told me to go away. I was just being friendly."

"You did the right thing," Ernest assured him. "The foxes are scared, that's all. As soon as they can have some fruit and nuts and mice, they'll be fun to talk to. We haven't ever had a fox here."

"Mice?" said Sir Walter, shuddering. "They *eat mice*? Like the ones Milly brings home?"

"Yes, that's what foxes do. You eat puppy chow and chicken, and I eat . . . well, I'm not fussy. I like corn bread in fresh milk the best, of course."

"And Gabby eats fruit," Sir Walter added. "I get it. But I want to eat sandwiches, like Grampa."

"Not good for dogs," Ernest said patiently. He saw how quickly Sir Walter was changing.

In a few weeks, he'd gone from being a silent, wounded puppy to being a chatty, active dog. A yappy dog.

To get off the topic of food, which was making Ernest hungry, he said, "Come on, Sir Walter. Our job here is to help Grampa. Let's welcome Old Man Musky. *Very calmly.*"

Sir Walter opened his mouth to bark.

"Wrunk!" warned Ernest.

Sir Walter closed his mouth.

Gabby muttered, "Bossiest pig in the world," but she joined Ernest and Sir Walter at the muskrat's cage. It sat in the corner where Grampa had first put it.

The big old muskrat glowered at them. "Go away! It's time for sleeping."

"No, it's not," Sir Walter said. "Nap time is over. I'm up, see?" He bounced up and down so as to be more noticeable to the muskrat.

Old Man Musky gave a ferocious growl.

"I beg your pardon!" Gabby said frostily. "We're here to greet you."

Ernest fidgeted. "Excuse me, Mr. Muskrat, we just wanted to welcome you to the Bed and Biscuit. Grampa will be with you presently. He's a doctor for animals. I understand you have a sore foot."

"What is this? Some kind of stupid ZOO?" the muskrat snarled.

"Not in front of the puppy!" said Ernest.

"I like him," Sir Walter said. "He's funny."

Old Man Musky squealed fiercely and beat his tail on the floor of his cage.

Grampa opened the door of the surgery. "Whatever is going on out here?"

"Yarp! Yarp! Yarp!" Sir Walter barked shrilly.

"Hush, all of you!" Grampa ordered. "Let's leave this old guy in peace. Play ball or something." He knelt down and rolled a blue rubber ball toward the corner.

The puppy crouched low, waggled his behind, and took off.

AnnaLee poked her head around the door of the surgery. "They ate it, Doc. That pile of mush is gone and they're lapping up the water."

"Good. Now we'll see whether they throw it up or keep it down. Be right there." He got up slowly, wincing as his knees creaked.

Sir Walter fumbled the ball, sending it smack at the muskrat's cage. Ernest hastily snouted it away. "Outside!" he announced before the muskrat could get upset. "Right now. Let's go!"

Thanks to the pet door, which Grampa had enlarged for Ernest, all of his family could come and go when they wished. Today, Sir Walter got busy outside marking several bushes, labeling them as his territory. Because he was still a puppy, he couldn't raise his hind leg, but he gave the job a sincere effort.

Milly sat up in her sunny spot to watch the small dog at work. "He's claiming the whole property!" she told Ernest. Leaning on her left haunch, she fastidiously groomed her right leg, all the way down to the toenails. "If that isn't just like a dog!"

"Of course," Ernest replied. "Remember that TV program we saw about wolves and foxes? They mark their territory, too."

"Quit preaching," said Gabby. "Let's play Guess Where Gabby Is."

Ernest called Sir Walter to come over so they could play their favorite game. The puppy was following an interesting scent and did not come.

"Wrunk!" Ernest ordered.

Sir Walter paid no attention.

Gabby and Milly called Sir Walter to come.

He ignored them all. Following his nose, the puppy had wandered across the broad grassy square, almost to the house.

"Bad dog!" said Gabby, who adored playing Guess Where Gabby Is.

"Leave it to me." Ernest jogged over to Sir Walter. "What's the matter with you?" Ernest knew he sounded irritable and he didn't care. "We have been calling and calling. Why didn't you come?"

"Because I didn't want to. I'm doing something else."

That's it, Ernest decided. *I've never trained a dog before, but it can't be that difficult.* "Sit down," Ernest told the puppy, "and pay attention."

Sir Walter sat.

Ernest fixed the puppy with a stern parental eye. "When someone calls your name, you are supposed to come immediately."

"Why?"

"Because I said so!"

Sir Walter cocked his head to one side. He didn't say anything, but he was clearly thinking. After a bit he said, "I am Grampa's dog, not yours."

Anger burned inside Ernest, but he waited until he knew what to say. "I know how you feel about Grampa, but he has the wild things to care for now, so we are trying to help.

"Do you want to be a good dog?" Ernest went on.

"I . . . think so." Sir Walter sounded unsure.

"No one likes a bad dog. Remember that spoiled white poodle who was here last week? He never came when he was called."

The puppy appeared to be listening, so Ernest pushed on. "Being a good dog is being dependable — being a good friend to your human. Are you Grampa's friend?"

"I am Grampa's wee laddie!" Sir Walter said. "His braw wee bairn! So sure, I'm his friend."

Ernest nodded solemnly. "And you'll come when we call you?"

"But you're not Grampa!"

"Grampa doesn't have time now! And you're supposed to come when Gabby or Milly or I call you. Is that clear?"

"It's . . . clear," Sir Walter said.

Ernest thought, *He's still thinking it over. He's not convinced.*

Gabby lit on Ernest's head. "Are we going to play or not?"

5
Tending the Wild Things

TO GABBY'S DISMAY, no one played Guess Where Gabby Is that afternoon or the next morning. Tending the wild creatures — plus the boarders and live-in animals — took all of their time.

Everyone could see that the wild animals were unhappy. They feared humans, hated wire cages and all the strange smells, and longed to be in their natural homes.

Old Man Musky was not only homesick, he was also in pain. Grampa had been forced to amputate about a third of his right hind foot to save the rest of that foot — and the muskrat himself — from a dangerous infection. Now the muskrat wore a wide collar around his neck to keep him from gnawing his bandaged foot.

Ernest sat by Old Man Musky's cage. "Tell me if you need anything."

"Go away."

"I promise you'll feel better soon. Give it time."

"Not going to get better. Going to die here in this terrible place."

"Not if Grampa can help it! This is the best place in the world. You are one lucky muskrat, Mister!"

While the muskrat kept a stubborn silence, Ernest could hear Grampa on the phone with his friend Joseph, the wildlife vet.

"Yes, I know Canada geese usually mate for life," he told Joseph. After a long talk, Grampa said, "Okay, I'll keep doing what I'm doing."

Ernest felt Old Man Musky's eyes on him, but all the muskrat did was make a soft *R-r-rrumph* sound, and then he sank into sleep.

Good, Ernest thought. Grampa often talked about sleep. "Nature takes over during sleep," he told people. "Animals rest and heal and recover naturally."

As he sat there, Ernest puzzled over their problem with Zeus the goose. Was the big bird getting better as he slept? *I wonder if he would talk to another bird, like Gabby?* The goose had now been at the Bed and Biscuit for over twenty-four hours, and had eaten nothing.

When Gabby finally arrived in the office, it was nearly noon.

"What's been keeping you?" Ernest asked.

"Oooh, it's a grumpy little piggy today." She shook her beak in his face.

Ernest squealed in anger.

"Look here," Gabby said, backing away, "you have your work and I have mine. The birds in our aviary depend on me to visit them. I bring the news—vital information about upcoming feedings. They need attention, too, you know!"

Chastened, Ernest lowered his snout. "I thought you were just doing the hokey-pokey for their entertainment."

"Honestly! The hokey-pokey is our exercise class! Do you want them all moping on their perches?"

"Well . . . no. It's just that our goose isn't eating. Would you talk to him?"

"Of course. You go get him some corn." Gabby flew into the surgery and lit on the counter near the Canada goose.

On his way to the barn, Ernest talked to himself. *And she thinks* I'm *bossy! Hah!*

Ernest went to the tack room in the barn where Grampa kept feed bins, a bin for apples, and his saddle and bridle for Beauty. Ernest got a big old pie pan in his mouth and scooped corn into it from the corn bin. Moving slowly to keep the pan level, he returned to the office.

Snouting the pan through the pet door proved to be tricky. Finally, by tilting the pan a bit, he managed to snout it to the inside. And then he

was inside, too, delighted with his dependable
brain for figuring out the way.

Trotting toward the goose in the surgery,
Ernest began a little song about his brain:

"Oh, I am a lucky, a very fine, plucky
young pig! For I have a most dependable
BRAIN!"

Well, it's a start, he thought. *I'll work on it the
next time I'm in the shower.*

Gabby was walking to and fro in front of the
goose's cage.

43

"I got it," he told her. "Do you think he'll eat it?"

She flew down and selected a few kernels of corn, which she dropped close to the goose's long, black beak.

The goose turned one dark eye on Gabby, then on the corn she had offered. He inclined his head, as if to say thanks, then closed both eyes. He shifted slightly from one foot to the other and settled his feathers for sleep.

On the floor below, Ernest heard only silence. No one moved. No beak scrabbled hungrily for corn. "Let's go to the house for lunch," he suggested. "Maybe he'll eat if we leave."

Gabby flapped down to his head. "All he wants is to go home," she said.

On the way back to the house, Milly and Sir Walter joined them. Sir Walter ran tight little circles around Ernest all the way to the house. "Watch this! I'm fast, huh? I'm fast, aren't I?" panted Sir Walter.

"Very fast," said Ernest, afraid he would either step on the puppy or trip over him.

"This afternoon," Gabby announced, "we're going to play Guess Where Gabby Is."

"After naps," said Ernest, who needed time off from being a parent.

6

Guess Where Gabby Is

WHILE SIR WALTER, Milly, and Gabby napped after lunch, Ernest went on rounds with Grampa. "Man, it's gorgeous out here," Grampa said as he tramped across the pasture toward Beauty, who was galloping to meet them.

Today Grampa rode only a short time before brushing Beauty and getting on with chores. Animals got fresh bedding very often, which was one of Ernest's jobs. Working with Grampa, Ernest delivered fresh water, feed, and anything else the animals required.

In midafternoon, Ernest jogged to his personal pig shower beside the porch steps. He pulled the chain and delicious water poured down on his head and back. Soothing water.

He began to feel like his normal, positive self, and so he went back to composing his song.

"Oh, I am a lucky, a very fine,
Plucky young pig," he sang with vigor.
"I can think, I can ponder,
My mind does not wander,
For I have a brain and it's big.
I'm a pig!"

Satisfaction washed over Ernest along with the water. The song about his brain was coming along, yet he wanted to work in something about how *dependable* his brain was. *Song is poetry,* he thought, *and* dependable *is not very poetic.*

Into his peace came Gabby, Milly, and the puppy, bursting one after the other out of the pet door and onto the porch.

"Let's play chase!" cried Sir Walter.

"Wrackkk!" went Gabby. "We are playing Guess Where Gabby Is!"

Milly, who often won the game, said, "We did promise."

"Okay," Ernest said. "No peeking!" The three formed a huddle, all heads in the center, all eyes closed.

Gabby hid in the dense, bright green foliage of a Japanese cedar. From there she called out, "Guess where Gabby is!"

After each of the three had guessed twice and missed, she declared herself the winner. She also won the second game, when she crouched in the deep grass by the cats' outdoor exercise runs.

Back in their huddle for the third time, Milly whispered, "Listen for where she stops flying."

Ernest strained to listen, but ears were not his strong point. His strength was in his snout, which was better than any dog's nose.

Milly's ears were better. She knew Gabby had crossed the wide yard and gone over by the dogs' kennel area.

Sir Walter had excellent ears. They stood erect on his head — perfect for gathering information. As soon as they broke out of their huddle, he cried, "She's over by that big hound dog!"

"Out of turn! Out of turn! He's supposed to guess last!" Gabby squawked.

"Yes, but he's right," Milly said. "We won this time, so ha-ha!"

"Yarp, yarp!" The puppy sproinged up and down with joy.

"Great game, everybody!" Ernest said hastily, before a fight broke out. "Now who's coming with me to the office?"

"Check out our foxes," AnnaLee said as the family came in through the pet door. "Just a few meals and already they look better. I named the bigger one White Tip for all that white fur on her tail, and I'm calling the littler one Bibby, for that furry white bib on her chest."

Sir Walter was watching the foxes intently. When White Tip made a testy little yip at the group gathered by her cage, the puppy yipped back at her — a small, fox kit yip. Looking pleased with himself, he yipped again.

"Time to move you girls outside," Grampa said as he left his desk. "Come on, troops. AnnaLee, as we go by the barn, please get that cage of live mice that's in the tack room. I'll take the foxes."

Behind the house and the red barn, several pens for animals and large birds dotted the grounds at the Bed and Biscuit. Grampa's group walked by these now-empty pens until they came to the one nearest the woods.

It had a sturdy, cedar-shingled roof, stout fencing on all sides, and one narrow door. Inside was a low, wooden perching shelf with a nesting box on one end of it. Pine boughs and oak branches leaned here and there, and underfoot lay a soft carpet of grass and mulch.

"I've stayed in cabins worse than this," said AnnaLee, setting down the cage of mice. "Okay, let's go." She shooed Grampa's family outside the pen.

Alone inside the pen, Grampa set down the cage of fox kits and opened its door. White Tip and Bibby shivered with fear.

"Here's a nice, fresh mouse to practice on," Grampa said as he let one go. The mouse saw the foxes, gave a frantic squeak, and hid under the wooden shelf.

"They'll never catch it now," said AnnaLee.

Grampa grinned. "Care to make a friendly bet?"

Sir Walter the Scottie turned to Ernest. "Let me in there! I want to chase the mouse out."

"That would be fun," Milly agreed. "And tasty, too."

Ernest felt that a teaching moment had arrived. "You would enjoy chasing the mouse," he told Sir Walter, "because you are a canine, like the foxes. All wolves, dogs, and foxes are canines."

"So I'm part of the fox family!" the puppy said.

"Yes, except they are *wild foxes*. You are a *tame dog*."

"I could be a wild dog! I'm tough!" Sir Walter said.

"You have to be *born wild*," Ernest said. "And anyway, what would you eat?"

Gabby croaked, *"Mice,"* and made the sound of someone throwing up.

Grampa chuckled and left the pen, heading for the barn. "Somebody around here has to milk the cows," he said.

7

What Is Wild?

AFTER GRAMPA HAD LEFT for the barn, Milly inched closer to the foxes' pen. "I can show you how to catch a mouse," she said.

"We can figure it out," White Tip retorted. "Anyway, how would *you* know? You live with a human!"

"We all do, and we're *very happy,* thank you," Ernest said.

Milly added smugly, "I sleep with Grampa, too."

"You sleep in the same den as a *human*?" asked White Tip.

"Grampa calls it a bed," she said. "And when I'm older and have kittens, I plan to have them in that bed. Grampa will be *so excited.*"

Gabby looked at Ernest. "More cats?" she murmured.

"One is really plenty," he said.

Bibby burst out, "We hate this place! We want to go back to running free wherever we want." She glared at the wire mesh of the pen.

"Do you have to take naps?" Sir Walter asked.

White Tip said, "We like naps in our den. It's warm and safe."

Sir Walter's head tipped to one side as he considered this. "What is safe?"

"Safe is when no one is chasing us — hunting us," Bibby replied.

"Who does that . . . and *why*?" asked Sir Walter.

White Tip stretched out, crossed her front paws, and spoke. "In the woods, we take care of ourselves. But humans hunt us. I don't know why. Sometimes a bobcat or a wolf eats a fox.

"A monster on the hard place killed our mother. She just lay on the hard place and died.

We were hiding, and we watched. Humans are inside those monsters, and we hate them."

"White Tip means roads," Milly explained. "The monsters are trucks like Grampa's, or cars, like the one I was in before they threw me out. I hate cars, too."

"We have a road," Sir Walter said. "Way up there at the end of our lane! Cars and trucks go by every day."

"Yes, and we DO NOT GO UP THERE!" Ernest bellowed.

"No need to shout!" Gabby flapped one wing in front of his snout.

"He's right," Bibby said. "We're afraid of the road place. Foxes are fast, but not fast enough to outrun a car-monster."

"I have heard that foxes are one of the fastest wild things," Milly said. "I see them in our woods, but they won't speak to me."

"Tell me more about being wild," said Sir Walter.

Ernest felt a quiet satisfaction. The puppy was being a perfect host, showing interest in their boarders.

The fox sisters stared at the puppy. "Look at us! *We* are wild," said White Tip. "We are free! You live with a human who is in charge of everything."

Bibby added, "We go where we want, when we want, eat when we please —"

"*If* you can find something to eat," Ernest grunted.

"That part is hard," agreed White Tip. "Our mother died before we learned how to hunt."

Milly shuddered, causing her marmalade fur to ripple from her shoulders to her tail. "I would be afraid all the time," she said. "When I'm hunting in the pastures, big hawks circle above me, acting like they want to come down and get me. I hunt, but Grampa feeds me anyway. Tuna fish is delicious."

"My mother died, too," Sir Walter told the foxes. "Right after I was born. Grampa is my mother. But being wild sounds exciting . . . and fun!"

With a loud clack of her beak, Gabby said, "I remember being wild. Way, way back there. Now I live here, and let me tell you, this is easier."

In the distance, a bell rang. "Oh, good," Sir Walter said. "Supper!" To the foxes he said, "I'll be back. And don't worry. Grampa always sends animals home."

On their way to the house, Gabby and Milly complimented Sir Walter on his behavior with the foxes. "Grampa would be so proud of you!"

Ernest plodded along in the rear, vaguely disturbed, but not knowing why.

Supper that evening was a party because AnnaLee stayed to eat with them. She had brought a huge meat loaf — enough for tasty leftovers — made by her mother as a gift for Grampa.

"Might as well put some on everyone's plate," he told AnnaLee. Gabby got a red pear, because she never ate meat. While they all enjoyed their meals, Grampa and AnnaLee visited.

"Doc, that Zeus goose is not looking good."

"Yup, I know. Of course, it's only the second day," he said, dropping his fork on the plate with a clatter. "I think this one is pining for his mate."

"So our goose needs his girlfriend?"

"She wouldn't be just a girlfriend. She'd be his soul mate. If one in a pair of Canada geese is sick, the other one stays right there and won't leave. If one dies, the other one can pine away and die, too, just like that." He snapped his fingers. "That's how I felt when I lost my wife. For a long time, I didn't think I could live without the other half of me."

AnnaLee gazed out the window into the dark. "That's so sad. But somehow you waited it out. Will the goose know how to do that?"

"I doubt it. Birds rely on instinct to tell them what to do. Our goose has a cage around him, and human beings. It's all foreign, so he won't get much help from his instincts."

AnnaLee reached for her thick red ponytail and began chewing on its end.

"I thought you quit that. Your mom said she had you cured."

"She keeps trying. But I go back to it when I'm upset."

"Well, you should prepare yourself, because we might not win this fight. Our goose needs to hang on a few more days, till I get enough antibiotic into him to kill any infection. Then we'll take him back to his pond."

Grampa leaned toward her. "Pass that meat loaf, AnnaLee. I need to keep my spirits up."

While the people lingered over dinner, Ernest — his stomach full and happy — dozed on his pile of blankets. Gabby snoozed on her curtain rod, and Milly curled in a ball on Grampa's lap, waiting for him to carry her up to bed.

Sir Walter lay in his basket. He had trampled the red Scotch blanket into proper position, yet he was still awake, eyes bright. The idea of being wild had enchanted his puppy heart.

8
Instincts

THE WILD ANIMALS had been at the Bed and
Biscuit several days before life settled into a new
routine. Right after breakfast, Milly and Gabby
checked on the goose while Ernest and Sir Walter
visited the foxes and Old Man Musky.

On day five, Grampa removed the wide collar
from around the muskrat's neck and replaced the
bandage on his foot with a slim wrapping.

"Look," cried Sir Walter. "He's eating!"

Ernest and Sir Walter watched the muskrat
greedily shovel in the fish, crayfish, and greenery
Grampa had put in his cage.

When the puppy barked to get Old Man Musky's attention, the muskrat growled, "Get rid of the dog!"

On their way to the foxes' pen, Sir Walter said, "That muskrat hates me."

"He just doesn't know that you won't hurt him. Wild animals often fear dogs as enemies. It's one of their wild instincts that helps them to stay alive."

"Do I have instincts?" Sir Walter asked.

"Of course. You know how you like to dig . . . and dig . . . and dig? And how you chase things and sometimes pounce on them? Those are dog instincts. Now, think about pigs. *We* never pounce on anything."

By this time they had reached the foxes' pen. "Hi! We're back!" said Sir Walter, bouncing like a toy on a spring.

Inside their pen, the kits cleaned their white muzzles after breakfast.

"I do that, too," the puppy said. He ran his pink tongue over the black whiskers around his mouth. "It must be a canine instinct," he said, proud of his new knowledge. "I love eating. I could eat all day long."

"At home, we eat whenever we want," said White Tip.

"Whenever we *catch something,*" Bibby added. "We always catch the mice that the human leaves for us. It's easy."

"That'd be fun, like a game . . . except . . . mice are yucky."

"Are not!" snapped White Tip. "Mice and moles and shrews are good, especially the little ones! And we eat berries, too—"

Bibby interrupted. "We need to go home now. Just open that door before the human comes back. We'll be fine!"

"Grampa will take you to a good place in the woods very soon," Ernest said. "For now, just eat and rest. Come along, Sir Walter." He nudged the puppy toward the office.

"But I want to talk to them! Just a little while. I promise!"

Reluctantly, Ernest left and went to the office, where Milly and Gabby told him that the goose was now drinking water. "Grampa is so happy that he's whistling again," Gabby added.

"What he needs to do is *sit down* so I can be in his lap where I belong," Milly said.

"Come on out here, and leave that goose alone!" Grampa called. Whistling contentedly, he sat down at his desk. Milly jumped up onto his lap as Grampa opened a drawer and reached for his phone.

Flapping fast, Gabby zoomed his way. "My phone!" she squawked, lighting on the desk and grabbing for the receiver.

Grampa stroked her head. "Feeling deprived, are you? Missing your little chats with folks in Vienna and Rome?"

"Bad man! Bad man!" said Gabby, who loved her games with the phone. For weeks she had randomly pecked buttons and waited to hear whether a voice would speak to her out of the receiver. If it did, she chatted as long as someone on the other end would talk.

After a couple of strange phone bills, Grampa had figured out what was going on. Later he learned that Gabby also answered calls when he was not there. She always pretended to be Dr. Adam Bender, of course.

One time, instead of saying, "Bed and Biscuit, how can I help you?" she had said, "Hotsy-Totsy Pet Hotel. This is Hotsy," followed by a loud cackle.

When Grampa heard about that—plus a few other sassy comments—he moved the telephone into a desk drawer. Gabby still had not forgiven him.

As Grampa and Gabby wrestled for control of the phone, Sir Walter charged in. Panting from his run, he said, "The foxes like me now. I explained about instincts and they think I'm smart."

"Is that so? Then they must be happier," Ernest observed.

"Oh, no! They need to go home. They're ready."

Ernest gave the puppy a look laden with meaning. "Grampa will decide when they go home. Is that clear?"

"But they said—"

"They're just babies, too young to decide what's best—"

Gabby hooted. "Hear ye, hear ye! The Right Honorable Lord Ernest Piglet—"

"Nobody asked you!" Ernest thundered, which made Grampa get up from his chair. Milly hopped to the floor, where she turned and gave Grampa a withering look.

"Ah, Milly-baby, I'm sorry," Grampa said, bending down to pick her up. "The rest of you, just toddle on out of here. I need to finish these accounts in peace. You can argue just as well out in the yard. And stay there, hear me?"

That day, Grampa lay down on the family-room sofa after lunch. Ernest felt that he, too, should rest. *I have to watch that puppy all day—do this; don't do that—on duty every second.* He heaved a sigh and fell sound asleep.

Hearing his snores, Milly woke from her nap in the kitchen chair and moved into Ernest's bed, snuggling warmly against his back. Gabby settled on the back of the kitchen chair for her snooze.

While everyone slept, Sir Walter slipped out for a visit with the foxes.

9

Back to Nature

BY MIDAFTERNOON that day, Grampa had decided to try something different. With the caged goose in a wheelbarrow, he led his family to their most spacious outdoor pen. "You're going to be a *new man* out here," Grampa promised the big male goose.

Zeus turned his head majestically from side to side, taking in the scenery, as Grampa undid the padlock on the pen. "Ahnnnnk," Zeus sighed.

Only Grampa went into the pen with the goose. "Get ready," he told everyone waiting outside the pen. "I'll bet this goose is six feet, wing tip to wing tip. I may have to hightail it out of here!"

Released from his cage, Zeus stood up and tentatively flexed his wings. Up. Down. Up. Down. He looked around and then squatted in the grass, wings folded. Motionless, he stared off into space.

Ernest slumped down, too. Next to him sat Milly and Sir Walter, and no one made a sound. Even Gabby was temporarily silenced.

Grampa's happy smile sagged as he contemplated the unmoving bird. "Well, dang anyway!" In frustration he took his cap off and put it back on several times. "I'd have bet anything . . ."

Gabby leaned forward, gripping Ernest's head so that she didn't fall off. "You! Goose!" she shrilled. "Shake your tail! Swim! Eat! Flap wings!"

She paused. "You put your right wing in; you put your right wing out—"

Grampa had to laugh. "Nice try, Gabby. Okay, folks, we did all we could. Let's leave him alone . . . see how he does when we're not around."

"Claws!" Ernest grunted. "Right now!"

Gabby let go and flew over to the goose's pen. When the others trudged back to the office, she stayed behind.

In the office, Grampa picked up Old Man Musky's cage. "I sure hope you like your new quarters better than our goose likes his," he told the muskrat. He snipped off the thin bandage on the muskrat's foot, and once again the family paraded outdoors.

The muskrat began a loud, nervous squealing.

Ernest went *wrunk-wrunk* in a reassuring way, Milly mewed encouragement, Sir Walter barked, and Grampa made soothing sounds.

Unhooking the gate latch, Grampa told the muskrat, "You're going to love it here. Dozens of ducklings have grown to adulthood in this pond and gone on to great things." He set the muskrat's cage in a corner, and scooted everyone out of the enclosure before opening the cage door.

Right away, Old Man Musky waddled out of his cage. He favored the wounded foot slightly as he moved around his pen, blinking in the sunlight and snuffling the grass and low bushes. He paused at the lip of the concrete pond, which looked like a midsize, round swimming pool.

Ernest eyed the muskrat's right hind foot, now free of its bandage. Where Grampa had removed the infected portion, there was a row of tiny, neat stitches.

Old Man Musky waded into the deep center of the pond and began to swim gingerly. His head high, he made a different sound — a low *snort-snort.*

Grampa broke open a bale of straw and put some in the muskrat's cage, leaving its door open so that it could be a sleeping den. "You can do your own decorating with the rest of the bale," he said before heading back to the office.

"That looks like fun," said Sir Walter, watching the old animal paddle across the pond.

"You'd be good at it," Ernest told him. "Dogs are natural swimmers."

"More of my instincts?"

"That dog asks a lot of questions!" boomed Old Man Musky.

Startled by the muskrat's sudden speech, Ernest said, "Yes, he does, because he's interested in you. We all are! Please tell us about yourself."

"If you insist," grumbled the muskrat, yet he paddled to the edge of the pond right away. "I shall begin with my birth," he said in a solemn tone. "I was the biggest kit in my litter of nine. I got the most milk from our mother and I'm proud of it. The muskrat world is tough and only the tough survive — and the fast swimmers who can escape the mink and otters who hunt us.

"We live by water, you know — burrowing into the banks of streams and ponds. I remember one time the mink came to our end of the pond . . ." He rambled on, noting which muskrat had hidden in which burrow, until Milly yawned.

"Am I boring you?" asked Old Man Musky.

"No, no!" Ernest said heartily. "It's just that we promised to help Grampa . . . uh . . . now. But I'll be back. Yessir!"

On their way home Milly said, "If Grampa only knew what we do for the boarders. You can listen to that animal all you want, but count me out!"

"Me, too," said Sir Walter. "I'll talk to the foxes. They have great stories, and nobody ever tells *them* what to do!"

"You don't say," Ernest replied coolly. He felt that his job as a parent had just gotten harder. *The fact is,* he thought, *a good parent* does *tell his child*

*what to do. I warn against danger or bad influences.
That's my job.*

His face wrinkled in thought, Ernest said,
"I'm coming with you."

Bibby was waiting for them, her black nose
wedged between the fencing wires. "Why are we
kept in this trap?" she asked the puppy. "We're
not sick."

White Tip joined her sister. "Would *you* want
to be stuck in here?"

Ernest listened intently, looking from the
puppy to the foxes.

"I know what you mean about running free,"
said Sir Walter, "so I'd hate it." He paused. "At
least the food's good here."

"Food is not enough," said White Tip.

Ernest saw Sir Walter nod slowly, thought-
fully, his eyes fixed on White Tip. Ernest gave
the puppy a determined shove with his snout
and said, "We must be getting on."

"But —" Sir Walter began.

"No arguing," Ernest said. "Soon they'll be back where they want to be. Only *this time* they'll be healthy and strong. Now we are going."

On the way back to the house, they passed Zeus's outdoor cage. Gabby was still there, gazing off into space, looking discouraged.

"Nice out here, isn't it?" Ernest said in his heartiest voice.

"Ahnnnk," moaned the goose, mournful as ever.

"Now, now," said Ernest. "You're outside! Smell the smells of fall!"

"Ahhhnnnnnnk," went the goose, his classic head drooping low.

"Oh, for corn's sake! Here we all are, worried sick, and you're not even trying to get better! Don't you *want* to go home?!"

The goose raised his head. "Home. Yes. Take me home." He looked at Gabby. "There. I said something."

"Rooty-ta-toot," she replied sarcastically.

"Mr. Zeus," Ernest pleaded, "*please* tell us what you need!"

"I need to go home."

Gabby sang, "Home . . . home on the ra-a-a-n-n-ge, where the deer and the antelope pla-a-a-a-y-y-y."

"Pond," said the goose. "Geese live on ponds."

"Home . . . home on the ponnnnnnnd," Gabby sang, very low.

Zeus cried out, "Why can't I just leave? I don't belong here!"

Ernest explained about antibiotics and taking time to heal from the arrow wound. "And you will go home! That's a promise. But you must eat!"

"Just let me go. I will find my home and my mate. Then I will eat, and she will eat."

And that's that, Ernest thought, realizing that the goose would not change his mind.

"I will wait," said the goose. He ruffled his wings lightly, as if airing them, then composed himself on the grass.

Ernest couldn't think of anything else to say. He was a tame animal who lived in a house with a human. The goose was a wild thing who lived on a pond with his wild mate. He had told the goose the truth, the goose had replied with his own truth, and they were miles apart.

10

A Bad Discovery

THE NEXT DAY was the sixth day that the wild animals had been at the Bed and Biscuit. Everyone in Grampa's family was tired because of extra work and worry. Most of them woke up late. And irritable.

Grampa muttered as he washed his face. "Poor goose, I know just how he feels." As he clumped downstairs he called, "Come on, Milly," but Milly hid under the bed pillows.

In the kitchen, Ernest listened to the bawling cows and wished that every day did not have to start with milking.

Gabby perched on the end of the breakfast table. Staring morosely at her bowl of brown rice and chopped egg white, she grumbled, "Health food."

Wide awake and perky, Sir Walter gobbled his breakfast, slurped water, and said to Ernest, "We should check on the foxes, right?"

"Wrong. Milking first. You know that. Then we'll check on *all* the wild animals, not just the foxes. Stay here until Grampa and I get back. If you get bored, ask Gabby to tell you some stories."

Beak clacking, Gabby said, "Oh, sure! Good old Gabby! She'll do whatever we tell her. Awwwkk! If that wouldn't frost your beak!"

Ernest and Grampa left for the barn, and while Gabby pecked fussily at her egg and rice, Sir Walter crept toward the pet door.

Out in the barn, Ernest and Grampa got busy milking. To keep himself awake, Grampa began counting. He'd discovered that it took about 340 squirts to fill a pail. Large, mature Holsteins like Ruby — his biggest cow — often gave seven or eight gallons at each milking.

When the cows had been milked and turned out to pasture, Grampa said, "'Long as we got such a late start, we'll do our boarders while we're out here." He began in the dog runs by brushing Sherlock, the bluetick hound, while Ernest handled the milk delivery, carrying the pails of warm, foaming milk to the house. One by one, he carefully set them on the porch. Of course, his shower was right there, beckoning.

Ernest positioned himself on the shiny white stones under the shower, tugged on the chain, and blissfully closed his eyes. As the water flowed over him, he thought, *A pig asks for very little. Regular food and a place to sleep, with water for bathing and cooling off. That's it.*

Unlike dogs, *who need a great deal of training, and brushing, and attention . . . and . . . where the hay is Sir Walter?* He knew they'd been gone a long time. The puppy would normally be outside by now, busily digging a hole or playing chase with Milly.

Ernest got a bad feeling in the pit of his stomach. Urgently he tugged on the chain to turn off the shower.

In the kitchen, the puppy's basket sat in front of the old black stove. The red plaid blanket was in place, but not the puppy.

"Gabby! Where's Sir Walter?" Ernest looked up at the curtain rod in time to see Gabby shake herself awake with a flutter of tail and wing feathers.

"Gabby! Wake up! Where is Sir Walter?" cried Ernest.

She peered blearily down at him. "He left just a bit ago. Went outside to do his . . . his business. Do you realize that your tail has come undone?

It is sticking straight out. I don't think I've ever seen that before."

"That's because I am upset! It's almost lunchtime. You were in charge! SO WHERE IS THE PUPPY?"

Gabby blinked. "Almost lunchtime? Are you sure?"

"My stomach always knows! Where's Milly? Maybe they went outside together."

Gabby flew down onto the kitchen table. "I must have fallen asleep. This is not good. I don't need a dog myself, but Grampa loves him and he's part of the family now. The trouble is, *you never know what he's going to do!*"

Ernest sank into a heap, disgruntled.

"M-m-m-orning," Milly purred as she entered the kitchen. She stopped, giving herself a long stretch, her rump in the air. "I feel so-o-o much better. Where's Grampa?"

"Outside," Ernest replied, anxiously popping upright. "Was the puppy upstairs with you?"

Blinking her emerald eyes, Milly said, "I don't think so. It's a very small space under Grampa's pillows. Besides, he can't jump up there."

Ernest stood up. "I don't like this *at all*. I'll go look for him, but I think he went to talk to those yippy, know-it-all foxes."

On the way to the foxes' pen, Ernest considered again the job of a parent. *Of course, I'm a pig, raising a dog. Maybe that makes it harder.*

Preoccupied, Ernest jogged past the muskrat's pool.

"You! Pig! What's the matter with this pool? I can't dig a tunnel!"

Ernest stopped. "I'm rather busy . . ."

The muskrat trundled over to the fence. "I said I can't dig a tunnel!"

"Really, Mr. Musky, I can listen later —"

"Now will be fine! In our tunnels, we create safe nesting areas for newborns. We also have escape tunnels for avoiding mink and the big fish that eat our babies. These tunnels are critical!" he growled, right in Ernest's face.

Ernest refrained from pointing out that this pond had no baby muskrats, no mink, and no big fish. Instead he said, "Well, then, it's a good thing you'll be going home soon to your own pond at the shelter. Right now I have to retrieve our puppy. See you later!"

He left the muskrat behind as he passed the empty pens and jogged toward the foxes' pen by the woods. Even from a distance, however, he knew something was wrong. No warning yips announced his arrival. No tiny black dog stood with his nose pressed against the fencing of the pen.

Ernest broke into an agitated jog, trotting all around the foxes' pen. He saw a tunnel leading out of it on the side next to the woods.

Stunned, Ernest trotted around the pen again, just in case he had missed something. When he came back to the tunnel, he snouted the ground and he knew. Two stinky little foxes and one clean Scottie dog had run away from the pen and into the woods.

11
Into the Woods

RACING TOWARD HOME, Ernest squealed his loudest, which was impressive. He squealed all the way back to the house, where he met Grampa on the porch.

"Something's wrong, isn't it?" Grampa dropped the dish towel he was holding and bent down to rub Ernest's head.

Still in full oink, Ernest pelted back down the steps in a most un-piglike manner. He looked over his shoulder to be sure Grampa was coming.

Together they ran to the small, empty pen nearest the woods and around the back of it to the freshly dug tunnel.

"Ah, dangit!" Hands on his hips, Grampa glared down at the tunnel. "Sassy little buggers! Dug way down under my buried fence. Just shows who's smart around here, doesn't it?"

Snout on the ground, Ernest began following the trail of the foxes and the puppy into the woods.

"Come on, Ernest," Grampa called, turning back toward the house. "They're gone now. I'll call the wildlife shelter and explain. We did what we could for those kits."

Ernest didn't give a corn kernel for the foxes, but they had to find the puppy before something happened to him.

"Ernest!"

For the first time in his life, Ernest ignored Grampa's call.

"Ernest?" This time Grampa sounded puzzled.

Gabby and Milly appeared, both aware that something was amiss. In a few short oinks, Ernest explained. Gabby flew immediately to her place on Ernest's head. Milly ranged out from him a few feet, hunting in tandem with Ernest, her nose on the ground, seeking the scent.

Grampa stood still and scratched his head. But not for long. "Laddie!" he cried out. "Laddie?"

Grampa threw his cap on the ground and called louder. "Here, Laddie! Here, Sir Walter! Come to Grampa! Come on now, come to Grampa!"

Ernest, Gabby, and Milly worked a bit farther into the woods. "They went this way," Ernest told

Milly. Behind them they heard Grampa calling for Sir Walter. His voice faded as he went toward the barn, back toward the house, and then over by the office.

Curving her ears toward the office, Milly stood still and listened. "How long is it going to take him to figure out what happened?" she asked.

Ernest, Gabby, and Milly had been following the crazy, zigzag trail of the foxes and the puppy for about an hour when they heard Grampa calling them.

Ernest raised his head and squealed.

Gabby flew off in a blur of green and purple feathers. "Do that again and I'll bite your ear!" she squawked. She made such a racket scolding Ernest that Grampa came straight to them.

"Okay, troops, I think I understand," he panted. "Ernest, are you hunting the puppy? Is he in here somewhere?"

"Wrunk," Ernest said, wiping his snout on Grampa's pant leg. He sensed Grampa's fear and shared it. These woods — wild and unforgiving — were no place for a puppy who weighed only seven pounds and thought that the whole world loved him.

"I've got water and a flashlight in my backpack," Grampa said. "I'll just follow your amazing snout and we'll keep hunting till we find him."

Long hours followed — hours in which Grampa and his family fought wild brambles that lashed their bodies, thorny bushes that whipped their faces, and biting insects that drew their blood.

Snapping at a big blackfly, Milly said, "It's almost snowtime! These bugs should be gone by now! Why would anyone want to live here?"

Ernest agreed. "This is a terrible path. Too much sun. Too many nasty bushes. Not enough shade trees." Ernest sat and waited for Grampa to set out the bowl with water. He knew he was overheated, a serious problem for a pig.

Everyone rested and drank water before they set off again. Grampa called, "Here, Laddie! Here, Sir Walter!" every few feet.

Evening came. The woods cooled off and the mosquitoes doubled their attacks. Grampa ran out of water, forcing them to go home for the night.

AnnaLee met them on the porch. "No puppy, huh?" She chewed on the end of her red braid. "After you phoned us, Mom and I called all over. Everybody knows to look out for him. We did the milking, too. We can keep milking till you find him." She gave Grampa a long hug, and he rested his head on hers.

"Thanks, honey. You folks are the best neighbors a guy could want. I'm just sick about this. When I think of all that puppy's been through . . ."

"You're sure he's in the woods?"

"Pretty sure, yes. Ernest and Milly seem to be following a trail, so I'm following them. I don't know what else to do."

That was a long, restless night at the Bed and Biscuit. Tense and eager for morning, Ernest listened to the clock hour after hour. When Rory the rooster announced the new day, Ernest was more than ready.

He jumped to his hooves, went to his private bathroom by the toolshed, then charged back indoors. Sitting at the foot of the stairs, Ernest gave a modest oink. When no one moved upstairs, he oinked again, louder. And louder.

Milly's feet hit the floor and then he saw her peering down at him. "Ernest, do you know what time it is?"

"Time to go," he replied. "Wake up Grampa. I'll get breakfast."

Ernest snouted open the refrigerator and the crisper drawer. He set out fruits, a head of cabbage, two tomatoes, a bowl of potato salad, and a loaf of bread on the food mat beside the water bowls.

"Come on, Gabby! Let's eat! The trail is growing fainter every minute."

"Ernest, do you know what time it is?"

"Time for breakfast!" he snapped.

A groggy Grampa filled a thermos with coffee and several bottles with water. Ernest in the lead, they pushed their way into the dense woods, heading directly toward the place where they'd stopped hunting the night before.

By now, Ernest's search for the puppy was driven by dread. *Do we have bears?* he wondered. *Coyotes? No, we'd have heard their howls. Wolves? Big cats? All of them could finish off Sir Walter with one swipe of a paw.*

I have failed, Ernest decided. *I am no good at raising dogs. Sir Walter was infatuated with those foxes. I should have seen this coming.*

"The fox scent is strong," Milly said. "Do you think that if we find the foxes, we'll find Sir Walter?"

"I hope so. But I wish we'd had rain recently. Smells are so faint when it's dry like this."

Grampa walked behind them, whacking his red cap against his leg and calling for the puppy. "Laddie? Here, Sir Walter! Come to Grampa!"

Ernest smelled the acrid scent of the fox kits, but the trail continued to be difficult. It would dart off one way, stop, then turn around and come back before taking off again in another direction. If they were deliberately trying to confuse a tracker, they had done a good job.

Milly sniffed the bark of a young fir. "They marked this tree."

By late morning, Ernest and Milly could detect only the fox scent — nothing that was Sir Walter's smell. Somehow, somewhere, the puppy's scent had vanished.

12
Following the Scent

AS NOON APPROACHED, they had gone over a mile into the vast woods between Grampa's property and the McBrooms' farm, where AnnaLee lived. Grampa went where his family led him. He drank coffee from his thermos now and then, but he said little.

Later that afternoon, Ernest smelled the foxes' scent angling back toward the fields of the Bed and Biscuit. This trail continued for a long way, to a small clearing shaded by Carolina pines.

"I've got him!" Ernest told Milly. "Sir Walter was here!"

Milly sniffed bushes and trees. "So were the foxes."

Ernest flopped down to think. "I have a theory," he told Milly, who sat in front of him. "I think the foxes ran wild when they got loose. They didn't care if Sir Walter could keep up or not. But they heard something that made them turn around and come back this way. Maybe it was the puppy, I'm not sure. But I get the best scent of him right here."

Grampa joined them in the clearing. He walked slowly and looked tired. "Do you all know we've been tracking for *nine hours*?" He sat down and leaned back against an oak tree.

Ernest moved over to sit touching Grampa. Milly hopped into his lap, and Gabby started singing, "How much is that doggie in the window? Arf! Arf!"

Grampa lifted Gabby from Ernest's head and put her on his shoulder. "That's a sore subject, you know. Our own doggie is lost! Plus a pair of foxes."

Ernest stood up abruptly. This was no time to rest! Not when he had just found the scent!

Snout to the ground, with Gabby back on his head and Milly by his side, he set out again.

"Gabby," he said, "do the *arf! arf!* part of that song, and maybe Sir Walter will hear us. Make it *loud.*"

"ARF! ARF!" went Gabby, who loved to yell.

Grampa, still resting in the clearing, called out as he had before. "Here, Laddie! Here, Sir Walter! Come! Come to Grampa!"

In between Gabby's energetic "ARF! ARF!" and Grampa's plaintive calling came a faint, faraway sound.

Ernest and Milly stopped, tilting their ears toward the sound.

"I think so," Milly said first.

Ernest aimed himself at the sound, moving at a trot. Milly had to run to keep up and Gabby took to the air so that she didn't fall off the pig. After a bit, they stopped again to listen.

"Awooooo!" came a small, pitiful howl.

Although he lagged behind them, Grampa heard and laughed out loud. "That's my boy! Here, Laddie. Here, Sir Walter!"

Everyone stood still, listening. Again came the same distinctive wail—a sound that only a Scotch terrier can make. It had not come closer.

Now each of them called for Sir Walter. And Sir Walter called back.

Milly's ears twitched irritably. "Everyone keeps saying what a smart dog this is. So why doesn't he come here?"

"I have a theory," Ernest began.

"Here we go again!" said Gabby.

Ignoring her, Ernest resumed trotting toward the woeful cry. *He can't come for some reason, so we must go to him.*

Ernest had jogged only a few minutes when he heard something coming toward him through the underbrush. The something alternately whimpered and yipped.

"Wrunk?"

Groveling on his stomach, Sir Walter appeared, his black hair filthy and matted with prickers, twigs, and leaves. Ernest smelled blood and saw bright red splotches forming a trail behind the puppy.

Ernest couldn't scold him. "What happened?" he asked as he snouted Sir Walter from head to tail. "Why are you bleeding?"

"I am a bad dog," Sir Walter whimpered. "I helped them dig so we could all run away and be wild. But I hate being wild!" Again he howled.

Ernest snuffled at Sir Walter's paws, which were torn and bleeding. "Did you do this to your feet running in the woods?" he asked gently.

"Yes. They kept running and hiding from me!" Sir Walter sat up. "They snapped at me! They said I was just a dog and should go home. *Just a dog,* they said."

"And then they ran off, and you couldn't follow because your paws hurt too much. Am I right?"

"AwooOOO," went Sir Walter, awash in misery.

"Well, now, a dog is a *fine thing to be,*" Ernest said, thinking that the puppy's mother would have told him that had she been alive. "Those foxes are just . . . just foxes," he finished, realizing that that was true. "They are who they are."

"Laddie!" cried Grampa, rushing into the clearing. He picked up Sir Walter and hugged him. He rubbed noses, tousled the puppy's matted hair, and cried a few happy tears. "Poor wee bairn," Grampa said. "Let's go home and bandage those paws. I'll bet you're hungry, too."

Ernest's snout led them back to the Bed and Biscuit. Grampa carried the "braw wee laddie," as he kept calling him. Gabby rode on Ernest's head, of course, and Milly stalked beside him.

"Leave it to a dog," Milly said. "Causes all this fuss, scares us us to death, and *he's* the one who gets carried home."

Ernest told her and Gabby what Sir Walter had said about being a bad dog. "He made a big mistake, but he knows now. He has a good heart," Ernest insisted.

Hours later, Ernest stretched out on his blankets, his stomach nicely full.

Grampa was bathing the puppy in the kitchen sink. He toweled him vigorously, then turned a blow-dryer on him. Sir Walter yipped and howled the entire time.

"Oh, hush," Grampa said. He brushed the puppy's black hair until it shone, then slathered disinfectant on his paws and wrapped them in strips of clean sheeting. By the time Grampa tucked him into his basket, Sir Walter was totally worn out.

"Sleep well, wee laddie," Grampa said, stroking Sir Walter's head. "And no more running off. Old guys like me can't take too much excitement."

13

A Good Day

WHEN RORY CROWED the next morning, only the puppy moved. "Going outside," he told Ernest and Gabby, "and I'll be right back. I promise."

Hmmm, Ernest thought. *What a good, polite puppy. I wonder how long that will last.*

In less than a minute, Sir Walter crept back into his basket, nosed his blanket into place, and went to sleep again. He was still sleeping when Grampa and Ernest went out to milk the cows.

After morning chores, Grampa phoned Terry at the wildlife shelter. "I know it's a Saturday, but is there any chance you could bring the van today? I have enough antibiotic in our goose that we could safely take him home."

Terry agreed, and Grampa phoned AnnaLee. "I hope you can come with us," he said. "We're taking the goose back. Pick you up in about an hour?"

By ten o'clock, Terry and the van were at the Bed and Biscuit. "I brought the county map, Doc. The pond's way down here, see? Sequoyah Pond."

On their way to the goose's pen, Ernest broke into a trot. Over his shoulder he threw a message to the muskrat. "See? Today we're taking the goose home. Your turn next!"

The muskrat blinked his nearsighted eyes at the group going by, gave a satisfied muskrat "Rrrumph," and went back into his straw nest.

Oinking with excitement, Ernest stopped at the goose's pen.

"Ahhnnnk?" went Zeus, his head swiveling left, then right, then left again. "Ahhnnnk!"

"Ho-o-o-me, home on the pon-n-n-d," Gabby trilled as Grampa halted a wheelbarrow next to the goose's cage.

Now he looked like a real Canada goose. Wings extended to their fullest, head high, Zeus flapped and flapped and trumpeted, "Ahhnnnnnk!"

When Zeus quit celebrating, Grampa surprised him with a soft black hood for his head and wrapping around his wings. "I'm returning you in good shape if it's the last thing I do," he said, grunting as he and Terry maneuvered the goose into his cage. They carefully lifted the cage into the wheelbarrow, and then into the van.

Grampa placed a blanket in the large, built-in cage inside the van. There he put Ernest, Gabby, Milly, and Sir Walter, where they would be safe in case of an accident. The van had two smaller built-in cages, empty today, and Zeus in his own cage, of course. Like any hooded bird, Zeus was calm and quiet. Grampa joined Terry in the cab, and they were off.

Only a mile down the road, AnnaLee waited at the head of her lane. She was doing jumping jacks as they pulled up.

"You have to ride with the critters," Grampa told her. "Only room for two in this cab."

On the way to Sequoyah Pond, AnnaLee reached her fingers through the cage to pet Ernest and Milly, then Gabby and Sir Walter, who couldn't seem to stop barking.

"Shhh," begged AnnaLee. "That's *enough barking.*"

"What did I tell you?" said Ernest, looming over the puppy.

"But . . ."

"Please," said Ernest, thinking how glad he was to be returning this wild bird to his home. Now maybe Grampa would have more time to train Sir Walter. A dog was clearly difficult to train, and Ernest wasn't sure he was up to it.

By this time, the movement of the van had begun to lull everyone except Ernest to sleep. Ernest went to work on the song about his brain.

"Oh, I am a lucky, a very fine,
Plucky young pig!
I can think, I can ponder,
My mind does not wander,
For I have a brain and it's big.
I'm a pig!"

Most satisfactory so far, Ernest thought as the van ran smoothly down the road. He concentrated until he could add the final lines:

"I'll sing loud in the wind
And rejoice in the rain
For my dependable,
Never expendable,
My dependable brain!"

The van stopped. AnnaLee unlatched the back door and helped everyone except the goose onto the grass. "Ooh, what an awesome place!" she exclaimed.

There on the banks of Sequoyah Pond, tall, brown grasses rustled in the fall breeze. Slender, dark green firs and plump evergreens rimmed the pond, with the occasional golden-leaf willow reflected in the water's glassy surface.

"Sizable pond," Terry said.

"Gorgeous place," said Grampa. "Must be spring fed to have water this clear. And look! See those geese over on the far side?"

"Let's get Zeus, Doc," said AnnaLee.

The men hefted the goose's cage out of the van and lugged it over to the bank. Zeus racketed around inside his cage and trumpeted "Ahhnnnk!"

Answering cries came from across the pond.

"AHHNNNNNK!" screamed Zeus as Grampa and Terry worked to free him from the restraining bands.

Last, Grampa snatched the black hood from his head.

Zeus charged down the sloping bank, calling at the top of his voice.

AnnaLee pointed across the pond. "See that smaller goose? I think she's trying to come over here! Well, she would if those big dummies would get out of her way!"

Everyone watched as one goose tried to paddle away from the group. Two large males swam in front of her and around her, heading her off.

The smaller goose gave a piercing cry and lifted off the water, flapping strongly toward Zeus and Grampa's family on the bank.

Zeus tried to lift off and could not. He lurched awkwardly forward, splashing water for several steps before his wings began working properly, allowing him to take off in ragged flight. All the while he called in a piteous voice.

The two geese met in the air, and Zeus flew one joyous circle around his mate. Together they settled on the water, close to Grampa and his family.

Now Zeus caressed his mate, crooning to her as she stroked him with her bill and sang low goose songs.

Tears ran down AnnaLee's face. Grampa and Terry swiped at the moisture on their faces and smiled at each other, wordless.

The three people and four animals beside the pond remained still until Zeus and his mate swam away, around a curve in the bank and out of sight.

"He didn't even look back," Milly said to Ernest.

"He's happy now," Sir Walter said. "Wild, like the foxes."

"He's home," Ernest said.

Grampa gave a gentle yank on AnnaLee's ponytail. "Maybe now we can get back to what we know, you think?"

AnnaLee giggled and patted him on the shoulder.

"Doc, I can't thank you enough," Terry said. "Just quit worrying about those fox kits. They'll most likely be fine. I'll be over to get Old Man Musky in a week or so."

"No rush," Grampa replied. "That muskrat is eating like a horse. Ernest keeps him company, don't you, Ernest?"

"Wrunk," said Ernest, rubbing against Grampa's leg. Ernest was eager to go home, where he could sing his new song to himself in the shower. Since he'd gotten to know the wild things, he had realized just how much he loved his home. And his family, of course.

Grampa picked up Milly and Gabby — the cat for his arms, the bird for his shoulder. To Ernest and Sir Walter he said, "Let's go, troops."

AnnaLee smiled. "A good day's work, like my dad says."

"All days with animals are good days," said Grampa.

Author's Note

CANADA GOOSE

In this book, the story of Zeus is closely modeled on fact. Years ago a wild Canada goose was found in my county with an arrow lodged in his neck. Our local North Carolina wildlife shelter cared for him and returned him safely to his home waters, where his mate was waiting.

Wild Canada geese live everywhere in North America, not just in Canada. These big birds congregate anywhere that offers open water and nearby trees or shrubs. Like deer, they have learned to share their habitat with people.

Adult Canada geese are impressive, with wingspans of up to six feet. Like most waterfowl, they eat aquatic plants, roots, young sprouts, and grass. Their bills have lamellae (teeth) around the outside edges that the geese use as cutting tools.

Canada geese live in families, like wolves, and typically mate for life. If one mate dies, the other mourns, often for the rest of its life. If the geese decide to migrate, they travel as families with the youngsters born that year.

RED FOX

The red fox belongs to the canine family, which includes wolves, coyotes, and dogs. Like others in this family, red foxes can run long distances on their long legs. They use their powerful jaws for holding and killing prey and their tough claws for digging and scratching.

The adaptable red fox, as well as the gray fox, has always flourished in woods and open country — all over the world — but they now live in suburbs and even in cities. If foxes know you can see them, they'll run away.

A vixen (adult female fox) and dog (adult male fox) can have anywhere from one to fifteen pups, or kits, who are born in the springtime with their eyes closed, like other canines. The dog fox brings food to his mate's den as she nurses their young, but he does not enter the den.

By the end of autumn, the kits need to be trained as good hunters, because each fox spends the winter alone. They are solitary animals and do not form packs the way wolves do. Even so, they enjoy communicating with their tails (a fox's "brush") and a variety of sounds. Foxes are beautiful, curious, smarter than dogs, and determined as all get-out.

MUSKRAT

The muskrat was named for its strong, musky odor, which is secreted from a gland near its tail.

The muskrat's heavy fur consists of underhair that repels water and dark brown, outer "guard hairs," which are also quite waterproof. They weigh about four pounds — only half the weight of a skinny house cat — but are more than two feet long, including their long, flat tails. This tail acts as the muskrat's rudder in the water, where muskrats swim forward and backward equally well.

Muskrats prefer marshy areas and are sometimes called marsh rabbits. Blind at birth like many mammals, the babies swim after only ten days and eat plants at three weeks of age. At a mere thirty days, these youngsters are on their own and will live about three years in the wild. In captivity, they can live ten years.

Although muskrats have weak senses of sight, hearing, and smell, they communicate well using a variety of squeaks and squeals. They are known as crepuscular animals, moving about only at dusk and dawn, good times for camouflage. Most interesting of all, muskrats have the ability to keep their bodies toasty warm while letting their feet and tails remain cool. This trait is called regional heterothermia (*hetero* meaning "several," and *therm* meaning "heat").